D1098366

ZEB
TO THE RESCUE

ADAPTED BY MICHAEL SIGLAIN

BASED ON THE EPISODE "ENTANGLEMENT,"
WRITTEN BY HENRY GILROY AND SIMON KINBERG

521 953 71 3

EGMONT
We bring stories to life

First published in Great Britain 2015
by Egmont UK Limited, The Yellow Building,
1 Nicholas Road, London W11 4AN.

© & TM 2015 LUCASFILM LTD. All rights reserved.

ISBN 978 1 4052 7626 9
59566/1
Printed in Singapore

No part of this publication may be reproduced, stored in a retrieval system,
or transmitted in any form or by any means, electronic, mechanical,
photocopying or otherwise, without the prior consent of the copyright owner.

Stay safe online. Any website addresses listed in this book are correct at the
time of going to print. However, Egmont is not responsible for content hosted
by third parties. Please be aware that online content can be subject to change
and websites can contain content that is unsuitable for children.
We advise that all children are supervised
when using the internet.

Meet Zeb.

Zeb is big

and strong.

Zeb is a rebel.

He fights for what is right.

One day, on the
planet Lothal,
Zeb got into a fight.

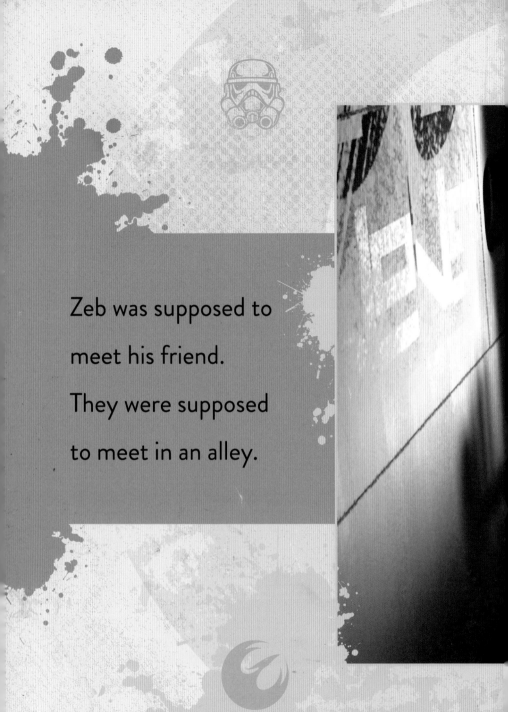

Zeb was supposed to meet his friend. They were supposed to meet in an alley.

But Zeb was in

the wrong alley.

Zeb saw a man and a droid.

They were in trouble.

Troopers were

stealing from them.

This made Zeb angry.

Zeb wanted to help.

Zeb used his strength.

He knocked their

heads together.

Zeb saved the man

and the droid.

Then more troopers

joined the fight.

The troopers

chased Zeb.

They could not

find Zeb.

So Zeb found them.

Zeb used his bo-rifle to stun

the troopers.

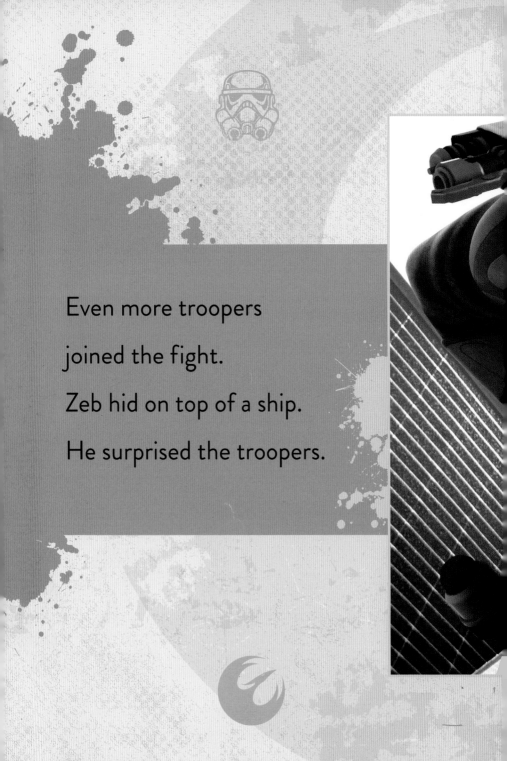

Even more troopers
joined the fight.
Zeb hid on top of a ship.
He surprised the troopers.

Zeb's friend Kanan kept asking

where he was.

Then the ship blew up.

Kanan knew Zeb was fighting.

The troopers

were no match

for Zeb.

The man and the droid

went to find Zeb.

The man and the droid

found Zeb in an alley.

They wanted to thank him.

They offered Zeb money.

Zeb took fruit instead.

Zeb was happy to help.

He was also happy

to fight.

Zeb likes to stand up

for what is right.

Zeb is a rebel.